THAT HEART BEHIND A BEAUTIFUL CHAOS

Dr. Sunaina Verma

ISBN 978-93-5667-242-0
© Dr. Sunaina Verma 2022
Published in India 2022 by Pencil

Contributors:
Editor: Nimesh Verma
Editor: Nimesh Verma

A brand of
One Point Six Technologies Pvt. Ltd.
123, Building J2, Shram Seva Premises,
Wadala Truck Terminal, Wadala (E)
Mumbai 400037, Maharashtra, INDIA
E connect@thepencilapp.com
W www.thepencilapp.com

Author biography

Dr. Sunaina Verma1

She is a Dental Surgeon, a Fashion Model (Winner of numerous Beauty Pageants and represented her state Madhya Pradesh in National level Beauty and Talent Pageant), a Martial Artist & let's be specific here that she isn't just a martial artist but she is a Black Belt in Taekwondo, an Artist (Got her first painting showcased in an exhibition at the age of 16), a Director, a phenomenal Dancer, a Boxer, a sports person, a fitness enthusiast, she has finished numerous Marathons, a performer, yet the words which truly describe her are FOREVER

LEARNER. She authored two novels "Wholeheartedly-For A LifeTime", "I Was Waiting For A Sunrise In Nevada", she also wrote a short story titled "Was It?".

From presenting scientific research papers and posters in International Conferences to hosting chill Podcasts and having a fun YouTube Channel of her own, from being a dance fitness instructor to making her favourite Italian dish.. she can make anything possible and if this wasn't enough then she also got nominated for the Student Of Merit- UG Award by her college principal in Pierre Fauchard Academy International Annual Awards.

But I won't be wrong if I say that this is not even half of who she is as a person, there is still an ocean of unexplored fields and a personality unleashed... Working hard, learning, falling apart and rising.

You can find her on social media by the following user names

Instagram, Twitter and Facebook - @isunainaverma

Youtube by SUNAINA VERMA

LinkedIn by Dr. Sunaina Verma

Podcast by "That NunChuck Girl Talks About…"

CONTENTS

Epigraph

Life doesn't always give you troubles,

but just in case

if it does

survive

& turn it into a memorable chaos.

- Dr. Sunaina Verma

Foreword

All journeys begin with a destination which you either decide or hope to reach at but it's never, I repeat it's never just the destination you decide to reach because the route often takes the clue and shows you how it can alter the path or even you.

I never knew a childhood dream of being an author would turn into a reality one day and I'll be able to share my piece of creative writing with people across the world. I started my journey without having a clear thought of my destination but this journey is juggling me between some amazing life events and *'That Heart Behind A Beautiful Chaos'* is something that came out when my life was juggling my route and possibly the destination as well.

Dear Reader,

'That Heart Behind A Beautiful Chaos' is a journey, I have booked its tickets for you. Get yourself some coffee, pack your bags and lets meet at the destination hoping for a place we decided to reach or may be at a place where we were supposed to meet. This novel is an outcome of my habit of building castle in the air which I would prefer to call creative thinking here so this story has nothing to do with real life people or incidences and sadly, I do not even have any magical powers to turn this fiction into a reality

so just sit back and enjoy the ride because we never know where are we going to end after this journey.

Acknowledgements

Dedicated To

My family, readers and all the well-wishers.

Keep reading & living.

❤

My Stunned Heart

Sauntering wind, soothing view, chirping of birds, sea water was reflecting the light of the sun just like a glass would do. I never felt so relieved before this, solitude never felt this soulful before, I was able to feel the calmness in my heart, this was the time when I realised that I'm ready to go back to the life that I had. That life which was filled with struggles, restlessness, dancing emotions.. Everything that a city life of an ambitious, self doubting youngster has or can have. I had all the troubles possible in life or at least that's what I thought I had. Life has always been a predictable rollercoaster ride for me. Everything that I wanted disappeared... Everything that I didn't want to happen, happened. I'm not a poet but I feel like..

Whenever I wanted it to rain,

It drained me.

Whenever I wanted it to glow,

it faded me.

THAT HEART BEHIND A BEAUTIFUL CHAOS

Whenever I wanted it to gloom,
it doomed me.

Life wasn't living,
Death wasn't deceasing.

How it can't be holding
How it can't be releasing

At last I don't know why..
Why does it keep repeating?

The rain, the drain
The gloom then the doom.

Everything just drained whenever it rained
Everything just gloom whenever I wanted it to bloom
My ambitions were fading,
My obscurity was rising.

Hence
Whenever I wanted it to rain, it drained me.
Whenever I wanted it to glow, it faded me.
Whenever I wanted it to gloom, it doomed me.

Alas..

Life wasn't living,
Death wasn't deceasing.

This deceasing life is mine but who am I?

I'm a boy at heart, a kid with my actions and a 60 year old when it comes to the number of responsibilities I have. I'm Anurag Kiran Singh Thakur. I know what you are thinking.. Wow!! Such a long & heavy name, but Kiran? Who's Kiran? Aren't Hindu people supposed to have the name of their fathers as their middle name?

Like girls use their dad's name as their middle name for years till she doesn't get married and after her marriage she changes her middle name from her fathers name to her partner's name like my mother did. All of her life she was Kiran Jay Singh Rajput but the very moment she married my father she had to change her name to Kiran Suresh Singh Thakur... I don't know why she did it or I don't know if she was bound to change her name or she did it with her will. All I know is my mother raised me with all the possible love, care, protection and everything that's necessary to raise a child. It's not like she was a single parent, my father was there... Well he still is but he was always caught up in his work life and now caught up in his news headlines. So I think she deserves it, she deserves being the middle name of my name all my life because let's be honest this is the least that I could do to appreciate her and choosing whose name you want to use as your middle name or not to use someone's cause you don't feel like so yeah I'm the guy who uses her mothers name as his middle name and I'm not a mumma's boy, I just appreciate her and love her.

Let's just get back to who I'm and why this bloom-gloom-doom scenario. So by now you know my name and why I use my mother's name as my middle name and that I'm all about you should get what you deserve in life kind of person. In addition to this I would say I'm not so studious, a bit of a workaholic, a little into fitness and so much invested in the arts kind of person. Arts here doesn't mean history subject arts but the art form in which you take papers, clay, scissors, glue and make something out of it. I know it's nothing that huge and I would be joked about because of having such interests but that is only going to happen if someone ever finds it out so I have builded my physique in a manner that everyone would just look at me and think that I'm all about muscles and focused on working out and shaping my body because let's be honest we live in a world which is filled with judgemental people. They prefer to judge you on the basis of how you appear on the basis of your looks, clothing and physique.

I have a typical huge group of friends who are into showing off of their looks, style and have that typical bad-ass attitude, so even if I'm the caring type its nothing that people notices because of my peer and people consider me the silent, arrogant type and I don't have to pretend or lie because of these personalities of my peers I'm hardly approached by people randomly in my college.

Apart from these personality traits and interests I think I would like to mention a bit about my family over here... In my family I have my loving and dearest mom who makes sure that I eat a good and healthy meal in my breakfast, lunch and obviously in dinner... She makes sure I don't skip any meal because of any stupid and random reason.. For her it's all about.. my baby should eat nice no matter if there's any earthquake in the neighbourhood or a tsunami in our own 500 metres of radius. All I know is that if I'm stuck somewhere in that tsunami.. she'll still come floating over a log of wood or whatever she could find and get me my meal and it's not like she's just like this with me she does the very same to my sister as well. I think most mothers are like this only. Anyway, moving on.. Now comes the turn of my always so strict.. into the details father who is all about putting all his focus into my life so that he can make me make it a huge deal then there's my grandmother who's completely opposite to my fathers nature and behaviour, I mean her focus is my health, my thoughts and all about how I feel which is exactly opposite to my fathers.. she lives in Bhopal with my cousins because she just loves that city because she has lived her entire life there only but she visits us in summers or if she doesn't then we just go her and try to convince her to come with us and just try to explore our city Indore and shift here but she doesn't and then lastly... my heart, more like my little monster and my go to person, my sister Trisha. She makes my life hell annoying but if I'm going through any kind of hell then she makes sure that I do not have to walk that alone. Sadly she isn't by my side anymore.. She left town and our home a few months back for her further studies to live on her own and get independent, also to become a doctor apparently. Can you believe it? My little monster is treating the monster in the human body and making them fit and fine again. Well! I'm gonna be so proud of her. Dr. Trisha Singh Thakur, my little monster. God!! Thinking of this gets me teary.

These four people in my life make my life worthy of living and feeling the privilege of feeling what having a family is and because of this I call my family "fantastic four troop". I know I can't turn into a huge stone, break any table with my punch, my mother can't get invisible depending on her mood, my dad..? well!! He can hurt you with his words wrapped in fire coming out of his mouth for you-me or anyone for their career choices and dedication towards their life. My sister, well she indeed has got some super power because that is the only logical explanation about her ability to consume extreme amount of food. Why else would I call her a lil monster? She can eat anything at any time and almostly anywhere and definitely everywhere.

What else should I tell you guys about myself? I honestly can't think of anything at this moment but if we talk about my interests then I would say apart from everything I mentioned before I think my interests would be photography of animals and moving towards the wild nature in the search of wildlife photography.

So my bloomed got doomed when one rainy night my car stopped working and I had to wait for my friend to pick me up from a route which isn't taken much.. not just ironically but in reality too because this is the place where people get robbed hence people avoid taking this route at night or in general but I wanted to get home quick and easy so I took this road and here I'm stuck so the route had no one whom I could ask for help or to drop me off to some nice place like my own house because if I do accidentally find someone over here to help me and ask them for their help they might just end up robbing me and leaving me to an genuinely abandoned place where if someone finds me they will find me in my inner clothes which is going to be embarrassing for sure and who knows if they might end up beating me too.

Oh god!!! I better get back in my car and lock all the doors before anything like that happens and where the hell is Animesh? I asked him to pick me up like half an hour ago… Damn no it's been 40 minutes already. Does he want me dead? Huh… I thought I better call him and ask him where he is and the moment I picked up my phone I saw headlights, two headlights at equal distance coming towards me. That could be the thugs who rob people over here on the bypass on two wheelers or maybe in a car they could be in anything but they are coming towards me.. Those headlights were getting closer to me every minute and they stopped moving at a distance which was not really far from me. Those headlights were of a car and they stopped right in front of me, I can't believe I'm going to get robbed. I was shrinking down in my driving seat in fear when I heard a knock on my window.

They kept on knocking and the knock was getting louder and louder, it was almost like they were trying to break my car windows… No, no, no I don't want to get robbed and killed. Godd!!!!! Please save me.

"Anurag Bhai!! C'mon open this damn door, Mar gaya kya?", I heard a sound coming from the other side of the door.

That voice sounded like Animesh's, I looked at him in a glance and jumped out of my car like a monkey asking him why he took so long and started blabbering like a maniac when I saw her coming out of Animesh's car and the world just stopped moving for me like it happens in all those typical Bollywood romance movies or may be I just got cold feeted at that moment cause I got awwwwwwstruck because of her beauty.

"Dude.. are you alright? Chal.. Let's leave from here, we'll get your car towed tomorrow morning, come.", said Animesh checking up on me to see if I was alright or not.

"Yes yes", I said in a hurry trying to not get noticed for how I was looking at her and how quickly my emotions changed and I got astonished by her beauty and lost every single thought I had in my mind at that moment. I took my bag, locked the car and moved with him towards his car and sat quietly in the back seat thinking of how pretty her eyes looked. Those eyes weren't of any usual colour, they were a bit of emerald green mixed with the greyish black colour of ashes, they had glance and shine of a finely polished glass, they were as deep as an ocean and not just the ocean, the depth of the deepest and darkest ocean where you can't even see the rays of sunlight reflecting.. That depth of ocean where you find red algae. She didn't even smile at me then, she just looked at me with a poker face, I mean how can someone look so mesmerising with poker face expressions.

I was sitting there at the back seat of his car thinking all these things when he asked me why am I so quiet and if I'm all fine.

To be very honest I had no clue what was really going on then, I was calming down my heart rate and at the same time I was awestruck with her beauty. I just nodded my head in order to respond to his question but apart from that I had no clue of what was happening. After that they dropped me off at home and then I just went straight to my bed, ending the episode of my shocked heart's roller coaster ride.

In The Search of Chaos

It's been a week since Animesh rescued me from my imaginary situation of armed thiefs & murderers on a highway which actually was just a punctured tyre and I'm still here getting stuck in the prettiness of those eyes every time I close my eyes. I want to ask her name, search her on Instagram and know who she is in person. What does she like? What she doesn't like? Her favourite food, places and songs. I want to know everything but I don't want to ask Animesh about her because what if she is his sister? What if he sees the craze in my eyes that I have for her the moment I'll ask him about her. I don't want him to realise that I just can't get over her one look.. that one look that drove me crazy.. so I just sat there, I mean here on my sofa thinking of her and staring at the wall.

[Phone chimes]

"Stop it you stupid phone its not like you are getting me a notification from the girl I like. Stop ringing.", I said and turned on the sofa hugging my pillow.

It rang again after five something minutes, it was Trisha..

[On call]

Trisha : "Heeeeyyy Bro… What are you doing this sunday?", Trisha started the conversation with Anurag in a singing tone.

Anurag : "Hi Anurag.. How are you? I called you to ask you about your plans this Sunday.. Isn't this a better way to greet your brother Trish? Don't tell me you forgot all your manners while living away from home.", Anurag responded to her trying to pull her leg with his sarcasm as an elder brother.

Trisha : "Listen! Stop! okay! Don't teach me how I should talk to my brother.", she said in annoyance.

Anurag : okayyyy.. Okay I'm sorry! I don't have any plans c'mon.. With you moving to a different city has made my life more still.. I don't want to sound like a dull big brother but you know I'm like that only.. I miss you.. I really wish if you could come here this weekend and we can have our fights like usual.

Trisha : Bro… That's why I called you.. I'm gonna make all your wishes come true like your true angel.

Anurag : Are you really serious, Trish?

Trisha : Yeah bro.. I miss you enough that I talked my Head of Department into some silly excuses and got him to give me a week off..

Anurag : you and your mischievous smirks. I can seriously sense that expression over your face right now.

Trisha : You're my brother, I know you are capable of that. Now seriously tell me you don't have any plans right?

Anurag : Haan bachhe zero plans.

Trisha : Great so I'm calling some friends over on Sunday and we'll have fun planning and executing a party on Saturday. Now I gotta go. I have some patients lined up, I'll call you back.. No… Wait.. I won't call you back. I'll directly show up at home.

Anurag: Cool!! See you pumpkin.

And suddenly I wasn't as down as I was before. I wasn't really thinking of how miserable my life would be if I wouldn't find her and tell her about how I feel without sounding creepy or like a random jerk trying to flirt. Anyways I got up from my sofa and kept on walking until I decided to settle the mess of my room.

Tired of the cleaning and settling of my stuff I ended up on my bed after two long hours, now I was looking at the round LED light of my fan thinking that everything that happens in life... happens for a reason and everything is connected to a series of events that ultimately make our life happen, be it a lizards life or a life of a human. Maybe I met her only to lose her and never see her again in my life or maybe it was because of my consciousness that I might lose the girl that I was supposed to end up with but who am I to judge all this? The Best possible chance is that I'm overthinking. We all meet thousands of people in our day to day life when we step out of our house but that doesn't mean that we are supposed to know every single one of them. The people we cross paths with on a road, the people we travel with in a bus, the people in a building working for different companies at the same time everyday. Ultimately I'm just gonna let it be now. Maybe she is just another girl I crossed my path with.

God knows what he has planned for me so I'm just gonna mind my business and focus on my usual life now. Thinking this I closed my eyes and only god knows when I fell asleep. Man!! I don't know what got me to sleep like that whether it was the cleaning of hours or the over thinking with a satisfactory conclusion of my choice but damn it… I literally slept like a baby.

So I put on my headphones, wore them, connected them to my phone and played my favourite playlist of some Bollywood songs of 90's & picked my brushes, canvas and colours to create something out with this relieved mind and soul filled with peace to pour my emotions and creation of my mind on the canvas in the form of a relationship of colours. One colour, two colour, three colour… It went on and on, all I had was an illusion in my mind that I thought would come out as a nice portrayal of my thoughts and be something deserving enough to be called an art piece.

I saw my mom coming into my room and just a few seconds later she came to me, pulled my headphones out, threw them on the bed and started yelling.. "Anurag, I have been calling you for an hour now, what's wrong with you? Why do you keep the volume so high? Do you really want to harm your ability to hear from this useless technology?

"Maa!! Maa!! Calm down, come sit here first..", I asked her to sit on the sofa in an effort to calm her anger and offered her to sip on some water from my bottle.

She snatched the bottle from my hand, drank some water from it, calmed her breath for a second and slapped me with love saying "are you seriously going to make your mother exercise like this.. climbing up the stairs in a hurry? What if I fall and break my leg? Is that what you want?"

"C'mon maa I want you to exercise but I would break my own leg before thinking of something that would cause you even a lil scratch. Okay?? You could have called me on my phone instead of this but what's the urgency?" I asked after answering her statement first.

"Yeah!! The salan is on the gas, we are out of salt, just quickly go to any shop nearby and get me a packet of salt, soya sauce and frozen peas."

But maa soya sauce? For salan?, I asked.

That's just something that we don't have at home anymore and I want you to get that now only because you.. out of nowhere asked me to cook Chinese food for you. Now will you get me this stuff? Or should we just order food online?, Maa asked.

Well!! We can order food online, I said and then mum's instant changing looks from calm to aggressive made me change my statement to 'Okay Maa.. Okay!! Just give me five minutes and I'll be back in a jiffy.'

Then I rushed to the shop nearby and bammmm I was in a state of shock after reaching there. It was her. She was right in front of me. Am I dreaming? Am I hallucinating? Man! I didn't know what kind of state I was in so I just decided to avoid the situation and move forward and finish my task as quickly as possible.

I moved towards the platform of the shop and the shopkeeper was sitting there on the other side of the platform, I simply gave him the list asking him to do it quickly otherwise my mom would kill me.

"Why is it always like this?", I heard her saying this, I couldn't recognise the voice because she didn't even said a word in car that evening but I thought or atleast I wanted her to be that girl only… the girl of my dreams and yes, it was her talking to me.

"Excuse me!! What do you mean?", I asked surprisingly with a confused expression over my face. I just wanted to act confused in a manner that I didn't recognise her.

"I mean why is it always like someone is after your life??", she asked jokingly.

"I'm sorry! Do I know you? I don't know what you are talking about.", I said in a manner in which I wouldn't look desperate or how much I'm in love with her already.

"Umm I came with Animesh Dada to pick you up last night, don't you remember?", she said in embarrassment.

"Ohhh!!! You are Animesh's sister. I'm sorry I couldn't recognize you." I'm pretty good at acting if she really believed that I couldn't recognize her.

"No we don't know each other anyway, it's okay.. I'll just get going.", she said, paying the shopkeeper her payment for her groceries.

(Phewww.. My aimless blank arrow hit the target, he is her brother..)

"Hey wait!! I'm sorry.. Please join me, my mom makes fabulous food and she'll definitely kill me today if I get back home alone.. Help me!! I already owe you one but please I'll be glad if you could help me again. Please don't say no."

She hesitatingly said okay and then we left to get back home.

I was on cloud nine. I had no clue how that happened and how the girl I was searching for just suddenly bumped into me. If it's not a match made in heaven then it's definitely a match made by my mother. I can't thank maa enough right now. I was so lost in my thoughts that I just didn't realise that she was saying something to me. 'I'm sorry you were saying something?', I asked her.

"I'm so sorry for your problem, how did this happen at such a young age?", she asked.

"I'm sorry? I'm not getting you?", I asked in confusion.

"Your hearing problem," she said.

"Wait!!! What hearing problem? Dude I'm fine. I don't have any hearing problems, I'm completely fit.", I said in a stiff and hurried manner.

"Are you sure?", she asked.

"Yes definitely, what made you think that?", I asked.

"Umm actually the incident that happened last night and right now the way you didn't reacted... I just thought.. I'm so sorry", she said and chucked.

"Arey!! Man right now I was just lost in my thoughts thinking if I got all the stuff maa asked me to or not and I won't prefer to talk about last night but as you have mentioned about it so let me tell you that it really is a very dangerous area and I was just being cautious." We both laughed because deep down we both knew what was the scenario last night and I was just hoping that she would be a sport and let that go and thats what she did.

And then we walked back to my home.

I introduced her to Maa as a friend and my future wife, obviously the future wife part of the introduction was in my head but yeah at least I told Maa this in mind.

We sat, talked a bit, and she introduced herself to Maa.. Her name was Aaira, wow I never heard this name before in my life it sounded so nice.. Aaira and damn Maa and Aaira bonded so well, their interaction was so lively after that we had lunch together and then she left.

Maa didn't ask much about her considering her as just a random friend of mine and then I went to my room and searched for the meaning of her name. Aaira means 'The Breathe Of Life'.. such a lovely name also her name compliments her personality as well.. she is so beautiful, she indeed is the breath of life for the people who fall for her just like I did and then I looked for her on Instagram and finally I found her. My search ended here.

Living A Lie

Approaching her is by far the most difficult plan that I have made, wait I would rather say the most difficult plan that I'm intending to make. I mean I don't know how to approach her exactly because she is… A dream and most importantly my best friend's sister. I think it's appropriate if I approach Animesh first. Well yeah I think it's a better idea that I should approach him first but before that I think I would rather dream about where I should take her for the next date… Our first date I mean, I'll also bring her a nice feel good kind of gift, a nice ummm what? Heels? But what if she doesn't wear heels, dude what kind of an idiot plans to give any girl heels as a gift on the first date? C'mon man I have to come up with a better idea. Maybe I should take a nap first.. It'll get me better ideas.

Wow! How I always know it's important and then I decide to sleep instead of working on it. Man!!! I'm so toxic.. Well!! I don't think its toxic, it's just procrastinating, delaying the execution with proper planning so that I can get to the work of execution of the plan after rewarding my body and mind with required rest for my body by a good sleep which could be a toxic trait for a girl who decides to end up with me. Anyways I better sleep now, I'm losing my reward duration. Which I clearly do not want to so Chao to my audience who are listening to all my planning and are assuming me to be someone amazing or someone dull or are just judging me, more like the way my retired neighbours who are dying to know about my life's haphazard situations and gossip about it with the other neighbours over a cup of chai and pakoras.

So jumping to the point where I overslept and got up at the time of dinner, after listening to some usual taunts from my mother because of a bit of oversleeping, I had dinner and for a sweet dish I called Animesh.

No….. c'mon don't get me wrong.. My interest didn't got changed but I hoped for his approval to approach Aaira so that the two of us can live together like a happy family and that approval.. that'll be my dessert, not just dessert more like a double decker chocolate mousse cake besides blueberry cheesecake with multiple muffins which have cute-cute icing of delicious cream with a tint of aesthetic colour and a cherry on top. In short it'll be a dream come true for me.

So I called Animesh with the hesitation of the whole world in my heart thinking what would I say and how would I make him like these feelings which I have for Aaira.

Ring… Ring..

Animesh: Han bro, all well?, Animesh asked after answering my phone call.

Anurag: Yeah bro.. All well.. I was wondering if you can drop by? We can have a game night and watch some movies later.

Animesh: Cool!! I'll be there in a bit. What's for dinner? I haven't had my dinner yet.

Anurag: The usual masala Bhindi with roti.

Animesh: ahhh! I love Aunty's masala bhindi sabji, I'll be there in a blink. Start heating up the food.

Anurag: Cool!! See yaa!

Animesh lives ten minutes away but he must be in his boxers right now so he'll get into his clothes, wash up his face, settle his hair with his bare hands and be here in about fifteen minutes and if not in fiteen minutes then in max to max duration of twenty minutes. So focusing on the plan I gotta make him stuffed with his favourite food and make him incapable of any fast movements so that he won't be able to kill me in the heat of the moment if he gets mad at me for having the thought of dating his sister but she isn't exactly his sister, she is his cousin sister, he doesn't really have the motive to kill me if I tend to have genuine feelings for his cousin whom he meet once in two or may be three years. So stopping with the possibilities, the plan is to make him over eat then make him play video games and lastly tell him after intentionally losing the game against him. Okay!!! 5 minutes wasted while calculating his estimated time of arrival and revising the plot of my plan. Now, roughly 15 minutes are there to warm up the food temperature, settle the video game scenario in my room, which is already setted because I play that all the time and this statement of mine proves that boys never really grow up.

After 10 minutes….

I was sitting on the sofa of my drawing room waiting for him to ring the doorbell, food was all set, I was prepared, I gathered all the courage of a lifetime in my heart to confess it to Animesh about my feelings for Aaira. Tonight I might lose my buddy for a lifetime or begin a relationship for an eternity. Let's see what tonight serves me after I serve him the food with the truth. While I was pulling myself up and staring at the door my phone rang. On the screen it showed 'Animesh Calling'. I answered thinking he might just cancel the plan, why else would he call me otherwise. Thinking this I answered his phone call… saying 'hello?, haan what happened? Aren't you coming?', 'Bro.. open the door', Animesh responded.

I opened the door, asked him why he didn't ring the doorbell.

Animesh: Bro… are you mad? It's 11:30 in the evening.. I didn't want to disturb your mom. She must be asleep by now.

Anurag: Yeah!! She actually is asleep. That's very thoughtful of you.

Animesh: Bro.. c'mon… your family is like my family. I grew up in your house. Why are you acting so differently lately? So formal as if you consider me an outsider here.

Anurag: No bro.. It's not at all like that. Actually there is something I want to talk to you about and I don't know. I think I'm just worried about the outcomes of that conversation.

Animesh: Just chuck it out of your mouth dude. I'm there. I'm your brother.. He said this and went straight to the kitchen, turned the gas off, smelled the food, took a plate from the third shelf on the wall, served himself his dinner, then came back to the drawing room and put the plate on the dining table saying 'shit!! I forgot to get a glass', and went back to the kitchen.

He came back with a glass full of water and put it on the right side of his plate and started eating his food saying 'Sorry yaa I'm all famished, I needed food so bad and this bhindi for me is like a heavy rainfall in the dry valley. Tell me now.. What is it that's troubling you?' He asked.

'Just give me a minute, I'll just be back', I said and went to the kitchen thinking it's just my friend, a friend who's more like a brother to me in my life. I have no apparent reason to hide this from him, these are my feelings and I can tell him all this straight without any hesitation because he deserves to know this and now I'm not going to hide this from him. If he won't like this or if it makes him even a bit uncomfortable I'll deal with my feelings for her and forget about her like she never even existed. It's not like I have spent much time with her or have been in a relationship with her for years. I have hardly met her twice, I can do this.

'Bro get me another chapati from the kitchen.', said Animesh.

I grabbed three chapati on a plate, took it to him and sat next to him. 'Bro.. What I'm about to tell you are my true and genuine feelings, I'm not lying and trust me if it makes you uncomfortable or unhappy I'm gonna let it go but I at no cost want to affect what we have. This bond of ours is really important to me.', I said.

'Dude!! I respect your feelings but I'm straight. You are like a brother to me', said Animesh with hesitation in his voice.

'So am I yaar Animesh c'mon, I'm talking about Aaira. I love her.', I said straight to his response.

'Aaira?', he said with mere confusion on his face.

Anurag : 'Aaira yaar Animesh… your cousin Aaira.'

Animesh : 'Dude, are you serious?', he asked with a wide smile on his face.

Anurag : 'Yeah… man I love her and I was so hesitant to tell you.. In Fact I was clueless about how you are gonna react.'

Animesh : 'Dude I'm thrilled to know about you guys… I love you both so much and she is just a perfect match for you.. I'm so glad you guys clicked but when did this happen and why didn't you guys tell me anything about it? Are you guys planning to elope before her matched NRI guy comes to India next month?'

Anurag : 'Wait, wait, wait!! When I said I love her by that I meant I love her, it's one sided for now. I have hardly met her once after you picked me up that night and then I just felt attracted to her so I tried to forget about it because I was clueless about who she is and how she is related to you but when I recently, accidentally, fatedly bumped into her in a general store nearby and interacted with her I just felt an undeniable connection with her so I called her here home to meet mom and even they clicked so nicely and then i felt like yeah! This is it. She is the one, I love her but before approaching her, I just wanted to take your approval because I didn't want to hurt you but what do you mean eloping, NRI guy and marriage?'

'Bro... bro.. Get yourself together.', Animesh said, trying to console me.

Anurag : 'How?'

Animesh : 'See firstly, it's an arranged marriage and secondly, you haven't confessed to her about how you feel about her yet.'

Anurag : 'So? What difference is that going to make? She is gonna get married soon. It's useless. My feelings are just gonna stay one sided.'

Animesh : 'Will you calm down? You are my bro. She is my sis. I know you guys and I want you to go confess to her about your feelings once because she said yes to that marriage just because of peer pressure from our relatives. So I suggest you approach her. She is going to be here for two more months and this is all the time we have. That fixed guy will be here in 20 days and you have to tell her about your feelings. You atleast have to let her know that you love her and about what she is missing if she'll just blindly marry a stranger out of annoyance. My sister deserves a man who is as amazing as her and we together are going to give her the opportunity to at least know what's waiting for her if she just stops for a second and looks around.

Entrance of The King of Planning

Doorbell rang.. Tiding, tiding…

It was 7 in the morning, Animesh and I crashed on the couch of drawing room discussing all the shit ideas that we got out of watching hopeless romantic movies which claimed that its always the true lover boy who gets the love of his life but after some planning-plotting to make the heroine of his life realise that it's him who loves her with all his heart and the other guy is nothing but someone who isn't really aware about her, her uniqueness and individuality as a being and by this only we had shortlisted some old school plans to approach Aaira. We both dozed off at around four or four and a half in the morning henceforth we didn't even heard a ting of the doorbell and mumma came running in the drawing room to open the door because of the continuous banging on the door and the sound of the doorbell. Mum opened the door and realised its Trisha and then I was there struggling to open my eyes looking at the door seeing Trisha and Maa hugging, they both looked immensely emotional.

Anurag: Hey!! You home…

Trisha: Yes. I'm home and you look dead. What were you guys doing the whole night? You guys look hungover like you have been living your life dehydrating yourselves with all the possible aerated drinks.

Animesh: Hey!! My baby sister is back here, Animesh said with a mild dozed off smile ending his statement adding "or am I just hallucinating?".

Trisha: Bhai I don't know about you but Animesh dada completely looks hungover. Seriously what you guys were doing?

Mummy: Is this how you talk to your brother Trisha? Apologise.

Trisha: But Maa c'mon this is how they look, just look at them.

Animesh: "Aunty we both look dead.. She isn't completely wrong but we wouldn't have looked like this if she didn't have rung the doorbell like a million times and banged the door in a manner where it felt like her intention was just to break it down.", said Animesh with a maniac smile on his face.

Trisha said "Shut up.", hugged maa and asked her if she could get her a glass of water.

The very moment Maa left to get her a glass of water, she picked up a pillow and started hitting us with it in mere annoyance, asking "tell me what you guys were doing yesterday behind my back or I'll just kill both of you right here bare handedly I swear." Meanwhile maa got back with three glasses of water in a tray when she saw us getting knocked by a pillow from the evil queen Trisha and then even she started yelling, "This is exactly what you both deserve, I'm sick of you both. It's good that now she is back, only she can get you both back on the right track.`` Then she sat on the couch laughing & if this wasn't enough she even started to record us getting thrashed by someone who looks half of her age.

"Okay!!! Okay!!! We'll tell you everything mann, please just stop now.", said Animesh.

"What? Shut up!! We have nothing to share here. We were just playing video games till late and got dozed off right before you started breaking our door.", said Anurag worriedly trying to cover up the fact.

"Maa tell Bhai just because I couldn't get time to spend here lately or talk to you guys often that doesn't mean that I have forgotten you people. We are a family, we have spent our entire life togethertill now. I know when you guys lie or hide things from me and it hurts, it makes me feel like I'm getting distant from you guys.", said Trish and started crying.

"What nonsense you both", mom scolded us both and started consoling Trisha saying," Beta stop crying, both these idiots are hiding things from me as well. If anyone who isn't a family here anymore then it's these boys. They have started hiding things and our family doesn't roll like that. You.. My sweetheart please don't sob because of these two, I'm disowning them right away. How dare they treat you like this? C'mon now gather yourself together, you're my strong child and what do strong children do?.``

"They let their emotions out but they gather themselves together and come out as someone stronger than before", said Trish while whipping up her tears adding "but they just don't include me in their lives anymore, I feel like an outsider."

"Hey!! Hey!! Hey!! I'm so sorry baby.. My actions made you feel like that, I had no clue this tiny thing would hurt you this much otherwise I would have never even thought about it I swear.", said Anurag.

"Even I'm sorry Trish, we won't ever do that again. Anurag and I will tell you everything.", said Animesh and hitted me with his elbow questioning "we are going to tell her everything right Anurag?"

"Yeah! We'll.", I accepted.

"You both better include me as well. This is my house, I can throw you all of out this house otherwise.", said maa jokingly.

"Yes maa.. No more secrets.", said Anurag in a lower voice adding "but you guys better get freshen up and grab some snacks because this is going to be a long story so I'm giving you all 45 minutes, manage everything and get back here otherwise no details.", said lighting up the mood jokingly.

"Sweetheart.. No details will turn you homeless. Okay?", said mum.

"Okay! Fine! Everyone please just come back here according to their comfort, whenever you guys can. I'll just simply spit out everything just like water comes from the tap. After all, I'm no human right? Just a robot with a play button around my neck.", said Anurag in sarcasm.

"Stop it everyone... We will all be here in exactly 45 minutes, ``said Trish.

45 minutes later

So that moment we all were there and there was seriousness in the atmosphere of the room, because no one knew what I was about to tell them that moment. I mean Animesh knew the sole reason behind that family meeting but even he didn't knew how I was going to put my emotions into words in front of the ladies of my family because you see you have to be very precise with your words and emotions while sharing it with the ladies of your family even though I have already told Animesh and yes! I indeed was nervous about telling this to Animesh but things are even more complicated here because I don't want to even say a single word that'll make the women of my family feel that I don't respect women. I don't want them to consider me as someone who I'm not. We all were there in the drawing room again, all the three of them were staring at my face waiting for me to say something and I was all numb over there. Gathering myself together yet I began with "so....".

"Finally... Thank you for breaking the silence.", said Trisha.

"Don't interrupt him, c'mon he just started.", said mum.

"Okay so I like someone.", I said abruptly.

"Really? Whom???", asked mum.

"You have met her.", I said, hiding my face.

"Whom?", mum asked again.

"It's my sister aunty…, he is talking about my sister whom you met a few days back.", said Animesh abruptly and ran into the kitchen saying "I need water now."

"Animesh daa's sister? Seriously? He doesn't have any sibling? Bhai if this girl of yours is imaginary then I'm sorry but I'm out I'm very tired really.", said Trisha in disappointment.

"Aye… Stay where you are. Okay.. It's my first cousin. She is real and this guy over here really and truly loves her. Otherwise you tell me, have you ever seen this guy this nervous or hiding his face from us because he is turning red out of embarrassment and blushing? Just look at him once.", said Animesh.

"Wait!! Isn't it the girl whom you bought home recently from the grocery store nearby and you introduced her to me as your friend. Isn't it? She is the one right?" Maa inquired.

"Yes maa.. She is the one.", I accepted.

Entrance of The King of Planning - II

"You lied to me Anu? Why didn't you tell me that she is your girlfriend? I'm not like other mothers who are old fashioned and don't approve of their children's choice of life partner. I'm open to your choice. That's very heartbreaking. You shouldn't have lied to me.", mum said.

"Maa...", said Anurag while Animesh interrupted me saying "she doesn't even know Anurag, aunty... It's just a one -sided thing.. He hasn't told her anything yet and she might probably get married to a stranger in few months & on the top of that, that guy will be here in about twenty days so we just have twenty days to turn this one sided love affair into a real thing otherwise she'll just marry a stranger because of her family's pressure. I feel so helpless right now. He hasn't even told her yet. I don't know how he is going to approach her with this lack of words.. The way he loses his ability to speak when it comes to her and God!! She might just end up marrying that NRI stranger without even knowing Anurag exists in this world. I don't know what to do now.", said Animesh and gulped down the whole water from the bottle in a blink and said "I need more water right now. I can't process this situation." & left the room again and went straight to the kitchen.

"Damn!! This is serious mann, these two people have nearly lost it mum." whispered Trish in mummy's ear.

"I know.. We gotta do something.", said mum in a hush voice. "You want to take the lead?", asked mum to Trish.

"With pleasure maa.", said Trish and went into the kitchen to get Animesh here in the drawing room. The very moment she got Animesh in the room he just ran but this time he ran to the washroom.

"I'm sorry Trish, it was an emergency… Couldn't hold it.", shouted Animesh from the washroom.

"Obviously!! With the amount of water you have gulped, I'm glad you didn't pee in your pants. Now please be quick and get back here.", ordered Trish to Animesh.

"Yeah.. Yeah.. Already here…" Animesh came to the room.

"Now as you guys have said that you both were planning something the whole night and this is why you both didn't sleep early. So tell me what you guys planned.", Trish asked us to tell her the plan.

"So see the plan is very amazing and trust me it is going to be instantly effective. So she goes to this one ice cream parlour regularly in the evening we will have our three to four friends waiting for her there, the very moment she'll leave from the parlour we will ask them to follow her and tease her and that very moment Anurag will enter like a hero and save her from that teasing and there we will have her looking at Anurag like a hero who saved her from goons. Amazing isn't it? This will definitely work. Amazing.. Right?", Animesh asked.

That moment Trish and maa looked at each other with a straight face and only God knows that their laughter that came after that was the loudest. I mean I have never heard them laugh this loud, they were literally rolling on the floor laughing. Evil laugh it was.

"I mean I just used to think that you guys have grown up to be some intellectual humans, definitely not responsible but intellectual ones but you guys still are kids.", said Trish.

"She is so right.. Are you guys living in some 70's Bollywood movie? Where some goons will tease her on the street and the guy who'll save her will win her heart. I mean I expected better ideas from both of you seriously.", said mum.

"What are you guys saying? We both spent the whole night discussing and we finalised this because this really looked promising to us.", said Animesh to mum and Trish.

"Do you have anything to say to support this idea of his?" asked mum to Anurag.

"I don't know maa… I have no idea what to do.. This is what Animesh suggested. He is very confident about this idea of his so I'm okay with it.", said Anurag.

"Aye now don't turn your back at me. You were also convinced with this idea of mine and now when aunty is asking about your thoughts on this you're like 'you don't know' what is this.", argued Animesh.

"Hey!! I told you that I can't think of anything to do in this matter and when you suggested I said I'm okay with whatever you decide. Don't be like this now.", said Anurag.

"Huh potato-potata", said Animesh.

"Shut up yaar guys, enough of all this.. let us think of something now.", said Mum.

"Mum you're on our side so can't we just go to them and let her family know that dada bhai likes her and we are sending them an official marriage proposal?", asked Trisha to mum.

"Point man!! We can do that na aunty.. Send home an official proposal..", said Animesh in enthusiasm.

"No dear… It doesn't work like that as he said that they have already fixed her wedding with some guy so we can't send a proposal for her now.. be it official or unofficial.", said mum in disappointment.

Trisha was roaming around trying to plan something.. When she saw some balloon packets on the T.V unit when she asked "why do we have this many balloon packets?", "I'm so sorry Trish, actually I was planning to give you a surprise party on your arrival before that party plan of yours but you came early and it wasn't even informed so it just got left there just like that."

"Oh!! party… On my arrival well umm hmmm not bad.. Actually.. damn wait, I got an idea..", Trish said.

"What?? Shut up! You must be giving some shit idea only.", said Animesh.

"Just because I refused your idea doesn't mean you'll call my idea shit, okay?", said Trisha in arrogance.

"Stop you both.. Okay!! Trisha tell us what you're thinking about? We desperately need ideas, it's not gonna be easy for sure and to be very honest right now.. any idea would be far better than what you both guys finalised last night okay? So here.. Trish tell us, what you have in your mind", maa put her heart out and showed us the reality once again.

"Okay aunty…", said Animesh and I just nodded my head in agreement.

"Fine. Now that everyone has agreed so here is what I have thought, see let's keep it like this that you guys are throwing a party for me.. Be it a surprise party or whatever but just some party in which we'll invite her and not just in the party but we'll try to involve her in the preparations of it as well so that we can leave her with bhai alone so that they can know each other better and then there, she might develop some liking for Anurag daa after knowing him... Hopefully.. You know we can send them for cake selection or some other shopping.. Basically anything that will give these two some alone time. What do you guys think? We can simply ask her to drop by to help us in the party planning, management and it won't even look like something that's made up or is happening out of the blue.", Trisha made her eyebrows bounce twice asking us for our views on her plan with her expressions.

"Well to be very honest… I think we can do this.. That isn't anything fancy or troubling, also there isn't any harm in throwing a party either. We can simply execute this plan and leave these two together as many times as possible. We can send them for shopping together or we can all go shopping together and leave those two here at home for the sake of decoration. I'm actually in.. This sounds like a plan, good job Trish.", said Animesh.

"Maa what do you think of this?", asked Anurag.

Maa took a pause for a minute and said "well!! This isn't a bad idea, we can do this… Also there isn't any harm in it. Technically we are just giving her a chance to get to know our man.. Right?"

Trish and Animesh nodded in agreement.

"But what if she senses that we are up to something?? She might feel that something is planned and we are doing all this with a hidden motive? I don't want to lose her.", said Anurag worried.

"Anu dear… You don't even have her in your life yet. Are you getting me? You need to have her as a part of your life first to lose her… Okay!!", said Mum, being the savage queen which she already is.

"Yaaar maa.. C'mon", said Anurag.

"Okay so I think we have two positive votes here for my idea. What about you Ani daa..? What do you think of this?", asked Trisha to Animesh.

"Yeah this actually sounds nice, we can do it and I'll just casually bring her here then Trish you do the rest like making her feel comfy and involved so that we can get her to stick around most of the time.", said Animesh.

"Yeah, I'll definitely make sure of that but what about her family…? Won't they try to indulge her? In random shopping and other preparation for the welcoming of the family of the groom and all other things..", asked Trish.

"What do you mean by the family of the groom, there isn't any groom yet..", said Anurag irritatedly.

"Okay!! Okay!! Calm down you.. The people who are coming here with the intention of getting their son married to the possible future daughter-in-law of our house. Fine? Sounds better now?" asked Trish.

"Much better.", said Anurag.

"You guys are too touchy, seriously, get a grip on your emotions," said mum.

"Sorry Maa!! Sorry aunty!!" All the three of us apologised together.

"Okay so let's end this discussion over here.. We'll make her a part of our family and if she feels like she can get settled here and have an ear that can handle this drama. Listen to your tasks now.. Animesh you'll get her here anyhow.. Trisha you'll make her feel warm and welcomed & you (mum looked at me and breathed out asking) what are you going to do is don't try to be someone else in front of her and talk to her.. Try to understand her better, give her a chance to understand you better then calmly and easily you can share your feeling for her with her and then we'll see if she reciprocates your feelings or not. Also we need to involve your dad in this plan too because he has been up and listening to all of our conversation by hiding behind the door."

"You guys never share such things with me, just because I'm your father that doesn't mean that I'm strict or I won't understand your feelings. I'm more fun, understanding and a chill kinda person as compared to your mother okay. I just act strict so that you guys can be afraid of me and focus on important things like education, work, life because of my fear but now that you guys are all settled in your life so I don't have to be that person anymore and your mum can loose the image that only I allowed her to have because one strict parent and one kinda chill parent match well for the upbringing of kids.", said Dad.

"Yeah uncle… We all are so settled that we all are here discussing and planning something so that he, our pretty little scared baby can have a probable love life.", said Anurag.

"Who got this barking dog out of his cage now?", said Dad.

"Uncle???" You're calling me a dog?", said Animesh in disappointment.

"Our family pet dog fool.", said Dad jokingly.

"Hahaha there we have a tit for his tat now…", Trish laughed and hugged Dad.

"So it's better we name this plan something now and I suggest we name it as MISSION : HEART TROUBLE.", said Dad.

"Papa heart trouble???", asked Anurag.

"Yeah!! Your heart is in trouble because you love her and her heart is in trouble because she is willing to get into a relationship with a stranger because of family pressure and our hearts are in trouble thinking about how we'll get you two out of this troublesome situation.", said Dad.

"That's witty now.", said Animesh.

"That's how I'm... cool, witty, amazing. Are you listening to all this praisings dear? Soon your days are gonna get over and now that they know how I'm, I'll be more popular among the two of us.`` Dad said this to mum and we all laughed.

Mission Heart Trouble

"Hey!!! Aaira… C'Mon get up we are leaving…", said Animesh.

"What do you mean leaving? Where do we have to go??", asked Aaira.

"Do you remember my friend Anurag?? We went to pick him up once late at night. He is having a party at his place so we gotta go and help him do the arrangements. Now c'mon hurry.. We gotta leave. There's so much to do.. The food, the decor… so much..", said Animesh.

"Woaaahh!! Hold your horses Ani. I don't even know him that well, what makes you think that it'll be a good idea for me to go there and help him with all the arrangements?", asked Aaira.

"C'mon aunty likes you, she couldn't stop praising you honestly and it is going to be a grand party so yeah we could use as many helping hands as possible.", said Animesh.

"Oh!!! He told you?", asked Aaira.

"He who???", asked Ani.

"Anurag…", said Aaira in a lower voice.

"No, Anurag didn't tell me anything. I met aunty… She treats me like her own child so she talks to me about everything, be it whatever then she told me that you and anurag bumped into each other at the grocery store & aunty was quite furious that moment so he bought you with him so she won't burst out of anger due to his deeds. That was fun.", said Ani.

"You guys seem to be pretty close.", said Aaira.

"Yeah actually we are like family only, they are closer to me than you…", said Ani.

"Ahaan?? Is that so?? Then you must be knowing him alot.", said Aaira.

"Yeah actually we both grew up together, I know how he is, how much things matter to him. How caring he is and his family actually treats both of us with the same love and care. Apart from paying for my education fees they do everything that a family does for their child.", said Ani.

"That's pretty amazing so umm this friend of yours must be having a partner.", asked Aaira.

"No.. Not really.. He isn't really into dating until unless he genuinely likes someone but why are you asking all this?", asked Ani.

"He seemed to be quite a nice fellow actually.. decent, good with words, like a gentleman only.", said Aaira.

"Ahaaan!! You seem to be quite interested in him.", asked Ani.

"Yeah!! I actually liked him but considering that they are your family so he must be your brother and according to that our family would want me to consider him like a brother only & anyway I'll be getting married to some stranger in a few months.", said Aaira.

"Shut up man. You can't be thinking like that because of this pressure from our family & you do not need to consider him as your brother. If you liked him then you should try to get to know him a little more before meeting that stranger. Maybe that's your fate to be with someone you like and ultimately get married to that person whenever you are ready to initiate that phase of your life and definitely not because our family wants you too.", said Ani.

"How does it matter now Ani? They'll be here in a few days and we know what's gonna happen next so even if I like him then he definitely won't be a person who would like to spend time with someone who is almostly engaged.", said Aaira.

"Just tell me, do you really like him?", asked Ani.

"Ani shut up. You're my brother.", said Aaira.

"That's why I'm asking you because I'm your brother and I care for you so if you like him even a tiny bit then trust me there isn't any better match for you than him.", said Ani.

"Why would you say that?", asked Aaira.

"Because last night when I wasn't here, I was with Anurag at his home and he wanted my permission to approach you. He was ready to get rejected by me on your behalf first and I have known him since so long, we have grown into adults together and trust me he never even liked someone but he is so sure about his feelings for you and now that I know that even you like him then how can I just sit here not doing anything. Don't you think you guys were destined to be together?.", asked Ani.

"Look Ani, I just met him, he is sweet, nice and all but it's too soon to be certain about such feelings. Destiny doesn't work in this way right? Destiny would have worked if I would have met him prior to this fasad and liked him then so this NRI drama won't have ever began.", said Aaira.

"See, give it an effort at least. Meet him then we'll think of something.", said Ani.

"Okay I'll meet him but it would be just because you want me to okay... I'm not promising you anything hundred percent. Also I'm warning you... You can not tell Anurag that I found him cute or you told me all this that he likes me and other stuff. Am I clear?", Aaira stated her side.

"Yes ma'am!! So let's go there now.. Shall we?", asked Ani.

"Yeah!! Let's go.. How are we gonna go there", asked Aaira.

"We're gonna walk.. Are you okay with that?", asked Ani.

"Cool.. Let's go.. Who else are we gonna meet there?", asked Aaira.

"See.. Aunty would be there, Uncle might be there but it's mostly his office so maybe he would have left, also yeah.. You know, Trish just got back this morning, she is also gonna be there, it's gonna be so much fun. She is a very fun person, you'll definitely love her. Her vibe is so amazing, you know she literally thrashed me & Anurag with a pillow this morning because she thought that we are hiding something from her. Haha it was so much fun.", Ani told Aaira about this incident of morning.

"Umm are you into this girl Trish?", asked Aaira.

"Aye!! Are you mad? She is just like how you are to me.", said Ani.

"Oh!! Okay!!", said Aaira.

"Give me five minutes.. I'll just change my clothes and be back in a bit, I don't wanna go there looking like a primitive human from ancient time.", asked Aaira for some time from Ani.

"Okie!! Then I'll also go, take a bath and be back.. Also have you had your breakfast? If no, then don't eat anything.. I told aunty that we'll be there in sometime so she must have made something for us as well. Also, one more thing... Don't tell anyone anything, if anyone here asks you where you're going then just tell them that I'm taking you out for a city tour.", said Ani and chuckled.

"Okay.. Sounds convincing.", said Aaira and left the room.

After 30 minutes of waiting for Ani, I got so frustrated that I just went to his room which was all locked so I started banging his door shouting 'Ani if you won't come out in a minute then I'll either break this door or I'll go on this city tour of yours on my own. Are you getting it?', 'Hey!! Don't... I'm almost ready, okay... Here.. Coming..

Just opening the door.. And here I'm.. see. All ready..', ' Dude I'm all famished, you asked me to not eat anything… If you are planning on killing me then please just tell me now.' , ' Hey! C'mon now you're wasting our time okay… C'mon let's leave.'. There we ran out of our house and reached Anurag's home running as if it was a sprint. I was all fine but Ani lost his breath. No wonder, these guys can just go to the gym , do weight training and pose showing off their muscles but a little bit of cardio makes them cry out from their muscles… 'Can't you focus on your stamina a Lil more than you focus on dancing with weights at your gym?', said Aaira in annoyance. 'Bro.. Cardio is for weak people, I'm strong. I lift weights.', 'Yeah I can see the effect of your weight lifting on your face right now.', said Aaira in sarcasm. 'Just step out of my way', said Ani & ran straight into the house for water and I just walked behind him when I saw Trisha saying 'are you a sahara desert daa? How much water do you really gulp in a day?' and I nearly bumped into her saying 'you must be Trisha… Anurags sister.. Right?', 'Yeah!! You know me.., you are far more beautiful than these guys explained', said Trisha & we both chuckled.

It was fun talking to her and catching up with these guys. I met Anurag's entire family there and they were all very fun and warm. Anurag also appeared exactly the way I considered him but it didn't looked like he has feelings for me, I mean he just looked like a nice person who was in the room with all of us but he didn't looked like someone who's having feelings for another person in the same room, he was all focused in the arrangements required for the party. I would actually just call him a good human being per se but not someone that I would prefer to be with to an extent where I'll go against my whole family to support my decision to be with him for a lifetime instead of that random guy whom I soon am going to meet. He could be wrong no doubt but then it would be a wrong decision of my family and not mine so in that case I'll just lose a guy who didn't even mattered but if I choose Anurag as my partner and in that case if anything there goes wrong then I'll lose him as well as my family which won't be anything less than a trauma to me. I'm gonna talk to Ani about it the very moment we'll leave from here so that he'll know my side and the reason of my decision. I was all lost in my thoughts when I heard Trish calling my name... so I responded 'hey!! I'm sorry, I was a bit lost... tell me what is it?', 'it's okay.. I understand arrangements get boring, you must be feeling weird that you just got to know about us and here we are including you in all our chores of preparation.. We should have just called you as an attendee.', 'No Trish, it's not at all like that.. Ani loves being here and honestly now I know why.. Because you guys just make us feel so warm here, as if we are a part of this family.', 'Hey! You are a part of this family already, you just have to decide the role you wanna opt here.', said Trish with a calm and welcoming aura of hers that made me feel so peaceful. She there made me feel so included in her family right there & that too just in a moment. Ani is lucky to have them, I again got lost in my thoughts and passed her a smile asking 'What you were talking about?', 'Yeah.. Ani daa and I were thinking that we both here will do all the arrangements, meanwhile why don't you and Anurag go out for shopping? You guys can get all the add-ons for the party, what so ever you guys think will be a good fit for our party, you guys can just get all that.', 'I'm okay with it but is Anurag fine with going out now? It's a bit late.', 'Don't worry about him. I just got back home this morning, I won't go out even if the world is ending.. Maa hates to go out shopping.. Dad is busy most of the time and everyone of us knows that if we ever allot Ani any work then based on research of our great great scientists.. the probability of that work getting done is point zero, zero, zero, zero, zero, zero, zero, zero nine.', said Trish and laughed.

'Oye.. Just because I have my own pace of doing things doesn't mean that I'm lazy or you guys will call me names.', said Ani.

'Yes sir, we know you have your own pace but we want things to be done sooner.. so Anurag and I'll go out and look for all the possible things that we can use in our party.', said Aaira.

'Oh!! Ummm okay but what are we gonna look for?', asked Anurag the very moment he got in the room and heard Aaira say that the two of them will go out for shopping.

'Anything that we think will be of a good use during the party.. be it food, something to add in decor or return gifts maybe.', said Aaira.

'Wooah woah woah.. Aaira we won't return gifts formally here.. It's gonna add up unnecessary expenses, it's a basic get-together that we are planning in the name of a party. I don't think we can spend that much in return gifts, because I don't think there are going to be any gifts in the first place so return gifts won't make any sense.', said Ani.

Trish nodded her head agreeing.

'Oh! Umm okay then return gifts are excluded from the list, so when should we leave?', asked Aaira.

'Well we can leave now, if now is fine with you.', said Anurag.

'Yeah!! Now is fine with me.', said Aaira.

'But guys it's 7:30 already.. Where are you guys gonna go?', asked Ani.

Trisha and Anurag's mother came and said 'Ani, they both are grown ups, they can go out and shop.. What do you mean it's 7:30 already?'

'Aunty.. How do you know what we were talking about?', asked Ani.

'I heard your conversation from across the room, you guys talk so loud.', said Anurag's mother.

'But aunty.. You don't even allow me and Trish to go get the vegetables past seven.', said Ani.

'Because you both don't know how to buy vegetables and those vegetable vendors can easily fool you both by selling you rotten tomatoes and vegetables.', said Aunty.

'Aunty you have no idea how savage and cool you are.', said Aaira and chuckled.

Both of us then left the house knowing that we were set up together for this and to be honest I was getting a chance to explore the city and Anurag got the chance to go out with me. It's not that I'm considering myself a trophy for him but as Ani said that he likes me which I didn't feel is true but c'mon it's a win-win for both of us.

The Walk of My Dreams

We were in the car, we approximately got five to six lanes away from Anurag's house, music playing in the car was soothing, it was a pretty route. I had no clue that Indore is this beautiful and has such scenic views. I was all lost in the moment when Anurag broke the silence and said 'We both are going to buy random things that will ultimately end up in the dustbin, you know that right?'

'Haha yeah I know that but that's all secondary for now, forget it. Focus on these songs, are you even listening to this playlist at all? These songs are just soulful and this route with such a view.. I don't even remember the last time I felt this calmness.', said Aaira to Anurag.

'Well I don't want to be one of those showoffs but this is my personal playlist which you are listening to right now & this is my trap route.', said Anurag.

'What do you mean a trap route? Don't tell me you're a psychopath killer, driving me to my death bed.', said Aaira sarcastically, hiding her confused situation because of Anurag's wordplay.

'No. I'm definitely not a serial killer, you can relax and lose those lines on your forehead..', said Anurag and chuckled, adding 'I call this route my trap-route because I only take this long beautiful route when I want an outsider to fall in love with my city and hopefully they'll refuse to leave so technically a route which has that magic in its wind that would steal hearts and make people stay.'

'Oh!! You want me to stay?', asked Aaira.

'I'm not certain about that yet but I definitely don't want you to leave Aaira.', said Anurag.

'And why that?', asked Aaira.

Anurag smiled and said 'just focus on the route for now.'

Aaira : 'Okay!! That sounds easy so I'll just focus on this pretty trap-route for now.'

We both smiled and focused on the route when after five minutes he broke the silence and said 'we will just park the car here' and pointed on to the corner of a road.

'Yeah! Okay.', I agreed.

Then we started walking and we went to like 30 some stores from which we got basic party stuff like some balloons, sparkling ribbons, fancy head caps, more like Charlie Chaplin hats but imagine all those in sparkling golden colour and after this Anurag and I came to the point where we both were famished and had no energy left to roam around at all so we decided that this much decor stuff is sufficient and we'll go somewhere to have our dinner. It was 22:30 already and I had no hope of finding any decent joint to eat but then Anurag told me about this night food street that is a night market of food and we can find every single kind of food there… From something as soothing to palate as cold coffee with multiple scoops of ice creams to something like a firecracker blast of flavours in your mouth. I got fascinated with the way he described the amount of variety of food that we were gonna get served there so I immediately agreed and asked him how far that place is… He told me that it was about two to three lanes away but it would be worth it to go there and that's a must visit place if you have a palate that craves taste and deliciousness. It hardly took us five minutes to reach there and I have never seen a place like this happening at night hours. Also, it was a place that had all kinds of crowds there at that time… families, girl gangs, guys groups, kids, elders.. I was able to see something so different that I hadn't seen before. That whole lane had a different delicious smell calling us so we decided to play a game, which was that he would turn me around with my eyes closed and we'll go to the place where I point and have one dish from the menu on which he points with his eyes closed, that's how we went and that was the best decision of our. For an hour we were there and there wasn't any variety of food left that we didn't tried.. be it momos, Chinese, Italian, North Indian, south Indian, we both tried it all.

After finishing every single dish that we ordered, we were running to the centre of the street and it was like firstly I stood there, closed my eyes and then he spinned me around after which I had to stop voluntarily and point anywhere with my eyes still closed. That's how we picked our first food joint to go to, it was a South Indian joint and after reaching there it was Anurag's turn so he closed his eyes and I held the menu card in front of him and then he just randomly flipped the menu card pages and pointed at a dish which was chocolate dosa. So this is how we got our first pick for the dinner and there wasn't any stopping after that, we were running in that food street like kids, next to this Anurag stood there and I spinned him around, he pointed at a momo joint and there I picked tandoori vegetable momo and we shared. My pick was better than his but there wasn't anything like his pick or mine because it was all the outcome of the game and we were having fun that time. We did this routine about eight times and then there was this point where we both were dozing off because of this overeating and lastly we just sat there on a bench in that street only. We both were talking and lost the count of time, that food street was so alive that we didn't even realised that it was past twelve and we were in the misconception that we were there for just about sixty minutes but we that moment we had lost the courage to move, we both were tired, the food & fun got us sweating profusely and those cold waves of weather made us stick to that bench but we decided that we'll move and get up from that bench in ten minutes and we putted a timer of ten minutes on my phone because it was already late, our car.. I mean his car was also parked a few lanes away.. right where we parked before getting into the market. We didn't realise but I think we walked so many miles that evening together that I must say miles walked with the right person is like that one blissful dream come true. All we did for those remaining ten minutes was to look into each other's eyes and that felt so peaceful.

Ting, ting, ting the timer rang and then we both laughed, it's time isn't it? asked Anurag. 'Yeah!! It is', I responded with a little smile on my face then we both got up after struggling to move. I must say I don't think that either of us will have this much food as dinner again for sure. Anurag at that moment succeeded in his struggle before me and then offered me his hand for support and I held his hand, we didn't leave each other's hand after that, all I remember was we were walking towards the car holding hands.

The car was far but this long route felt calm but this calmness wasn't for long, before we realised there were three middle aged guys following the two of us. We felt that we heard some continuous footsteps other than ours and their speed were changing as we were changing ours. Anurag got close to me, flipped my hair and putted them behind my left ear and whispered in my ear asking 'do you have a pepper spray?', I immediately nodded my head in a no and he pulled me a lil more close and whispered again 'don't panic, act normal okay.. we are getting followed. We need to act smart, our car is in the next lane so run on the count of three.' The very moment he said this, I nodded my head vertically and we gripped our holding hands tighter. Anurag started the countdown to three, two, one… and we ran so fast. We felt like we left those goons behind or whoever they were but we were wrong, one of those goons was able to catch us and he was standing right right behind us there. Anurag took a few steps saying Aaira get into the car now and he opened the car through the key in his pocket and told that goon that 'brother.. We don't want any trouble, okay? We don't know you, this never happened and we are just leaving from here.' I didn't got in the car that moment and then that goon started getting close to Anurag saying 'I wish you didn't but now you have seen me and I'm not going to let you forget this..', he said this and came running towards Anurag in an attempt to hit him and knock him down but damn Anurag dugged down and punched him on his body of mandible… I couldn't trust my eyes but he knocked him down there but that time wasn't ours.. those remaining two goons got there that moment only but before they could reach us Anurag and I got in the car and drove so fast. I was continuously looking behind to check whether they were following us or not. Anurag was driving really fast and after five six lanes and I sighed in relief, finally sat properly. I think we digested all the junk we ate, said Anurag and we both laughed tremendously. 'God!! I honestly felt every single possible emotion tonight, I don't wanna feel another rise in my heartbeat.'

'Are you sure that you felt every single emotion?', asked Anurag.

Aaira : 'Yeah!! I guess..', I told Anurag in a confused tone because I knew where this was going to get.

'Did you feel the emotion of love by any chance?', Anurag asked in a lower voice.

Aaira : 'I don't think I'm bound to answer this to you Anurag c'mon.' I said and chuckled.

Anurag : 'Well you aren't bound to answer me anything but I would be really thankful to you if you do answer this before that guy who's supposed to marry you shows up here. You know we can save his flight expenses this way, travelling from one country to another isn't a usual fare.. In Indian rupees it would be a five to six digit number.'

Aaira : 'If I say that I don't feel the same to what I felt prior to this adventure outing of ours then what would you say?'

Anurag : 'I would say.. I hope you hated me prior to this trip then..'

Aaira : 'You aren't someone who would step back easily. Isn't it?'

Anurag : 'Well!! We just ran for saving our lives, we never know what the next minute holds for us so if I wanna ask you things directly to avoid any haphazard situation of overthinking or presuming then you can call me stubborn but I am not letting go of the feelings that I felt just like that, without even knowing your part.'

Aaira : 'So maybe I like you, maybe I don't like you, maybe we can be a thing together and have a happy life but the reality is that we have reached home and even if this was the best and most craziest evening that I have had in my life but I'm getting married to someone and that isn't you. I also see everyone trying to make us turn into something and who knows that probably that is for the best as so many people are putting efforts on this and not just from your side but mine too yet I'm bound in a commitment that I didn't made and honestly I can't even back out of it now.'

Anurag : 'Forget about all this for a minute Aaira, forget about the commitment that your family made and tell me straight, we have just spent some time together yet do you feel like we can have a thing together… a thing that might last forever.. Can you see that happening?'

Aaira : 'Yes. Now what?'

Anurag : 'I don't know, I'm just happy that it's mutual.'

Aaira : 'That's it? All this intense conversation just to end the discussion with that you don't know?'

Anurag : 'No. It's not that. Let's talk about it tomorrow.. Can we?'

'Fine.. nothing is left to lose now anyway.' I said and got out of the car.

Above Everything

He dropped me at Ani's house only and I don't know why but there was this hustle-bustle in the house that I was able to hear from outside the main door only. I was confused but there were so many thoughts in my mind at that moment that I preferred to avoid that scenario at that point but I didn't even know that these thoughts were about to get more complicated than I ever thought. Ani's mother opened the door and I asked her what's this flurry all about. She asked me to just get in first and all I could see was n-number of people over there. A crazy amount of snacks were served on the table with four to five different kinds of sweets. I was stunned with what I saw there... It was Sampat sitting there with his family. I was stunned there, what got him here? He was supposed to come after somedays, not today.

He looked all fine and excited with everything going on around. Everyone asked me to sit next to him and have something from the food served to him and his family. I was processing all this with the time that I had just spent with Anurag when my family just pulled me and made me sit next to him and then what happened was beyond my imagination. He got close to me and whispered in my ear 'How was your evening? I hope your friend didn't turn into broken pieces.' and chuckled. I was clueless about everything already and now this? How he got to know about that incident if he just landed here from another country. How can he be aware about this situation and even if he heard this from someone then too there isn't anything to joke about it.. Anurag and I were literally running to save our life and dodge all kinds of probabilities of us ending up in trouble. I wasn't even in a situation to question him here with everyone around about this because everyone here thought Ani daa took me out to show me town. I just sat there quietly for everyone to go to their rooms and settle down so that I could ask Sampat about all this.

They took about an hour to get scattered but when they did I couldn't wait but ask Sampat how he knew all this. He was just sitting there all calm as if nothing happened, it was a disastrous situation.. anything could have happened and if he's aware then he should be concerned and worried but he is all fine sitting here and eating all the snacks. I couldn't wait any longer so I broke the silence and asked him straight 'Sampat how do you know about this evening?'

Sampat : 'What do you think Aaira, who am I?'

Aaira : 'That's not the answer to my question. I have asked you something Sampat, c'mon answer me.'

Sampat : 'Calm down Aaira.. This isn't our place exactly.. it's your relatives house, lower your voice.. I don't think you wanna create a scene here. Don't you think that they won't like the fact that you were out roaming around the city with a random guy whom you met a few days back only.'

Aaira : 'Sampat please… answer me..'

Sampat : 'See Aaira, it's basic.. you run a background check on people whom you wanna make a part of your family but in cases like mine? We need to let our people follow and keep an eye on people we are willing to connect with.'

Aaira : 'What do you mean? What people? What's all this?'

Sampat : 'Okay! What do you think I do in my life Aaira?'

Aaira : 'You are a businessman… you own your business empire.'

Sampat : 'Yes!! That is true and I built it on my own but this isn't my first source of income or the only reason of respect that I have today.'

Aaira : 'What do you mean?'

Sampat : 'I mean I don't wanna put it in an arrogant way but I'm the king Aaira. I own what I like and whoever I want. If I can rule a country that isn't even something that I would call mine then what makes you think that I can't control this city?'

Aaira : 'Who are you exactly Sampat?'

Sampat : 'For you? Your soon to be a husband, just remember this. Also, those goons weren't behind you. I just don't think you should meet some guy like that, I wouldn't like my wife to go out with such random people. Okay? C'mon Aaira say yes. It's our family who wants us to spend the rest of our lives together, they got me in your life and I don't know about you but I do listen to my parents commands and obey them. Also what happened today was more like a trailer for him and definitely a lesson for my lil Animesh. I'm having a bit of a jetlag situation here so I'll just leave you here to think about your mistakes, you can't undo them but yeah you can focus on how you would avoid such situations later on in your life. See you in the morning wifey.'

Aaira : 'Sampat.. that's not the answer to my question.'

Sampat : 'Oh sorry!! This isn't? Ask me again.'

Aaira : 'Did you hire people to keep an eye on me?'

Sampat : 'No. I didn't hire anyone.'

Aaira : 'Then who were those people?'

Sampat : 'Those are the people who owe me their lives and are bound to follow my commands.'

Aaira : 'So you asked them to attack me and my friend.'

Sampat : 'No. I didn't ask them to do that.'

Aaira : 'Then how did you know what happened and what and why do those people owe you?'

Sampat : 'See Aaira I have a past that I have left behind but I cannot let go of that past and there are people whom I have forgiven and for that forgiveness they have surrendered themselves to me.' He came right in front of me looking me in my eyes and said this, adding to this he also said 'Aaira I'm here to spend the rest of my life with you which means I see my future with you already and I do not want my past to scare you.. respect my privacy as I'm respecting your past and privacy. What happened was because that guy was trying to get close to you, that's it.'

Aaira : 'Since how long have you been watching me like this? With those slaves of yours…'

Sampat : 'I'm not keeping an eye on you Aaira, those people follow you to protect you from people who can harm you.'

Aaira : 'There's no-one who wants to harm me apart from you.'

Sampat : 'There are people who want to hurt me and now that I have made you a part of my life they might try to hurt you as well and I'm never gonna let that happen.'

Aaira : 'Is this some kind of cheap act to portray your power?'

Sampat : 'Just care.. nothing else and it'll be the best for you to accept it at the earliest so that you can adapt to it sooner because we are going to marry by the end of this month so I'm giving you one day to get rid of all these random people who are just wasting your time… Okay? Now I'll leave you here so that you can sit here and start accepting this at the earliest. Good night my dear.'

And I just stood there, blank.. because this guy over here is some really big influential shit or just some lafantar who's acting like a big thing.. I have no clue what my family has pushed me into.. I have to do a background check on my own now.. I was all confused and stunned when Animesh walked in with Trish and asked me what happened, I told them everything and then we sat there all clueless.

Trisha just got up from the couch in a hurry and started looking for something, after two minutes of her haphazard searching Animesh finally asked her what she was looking for? I forgot my phone, I need to search for something online... Where is your laptop?

'Trish.. search it over my phone for now, there are so many people here in this house right now and this noise pollution you are creating for this search mission of yours will disturb all of them.', said Animesh.

'Yeah.. sorry!!', said Trish and took Animesh's phone.

I was just sitting there and watching all this happening when she jumped and shouted with confidence 'I knew it's him'. 'Who is whom?', asked Animesh.

'Here.. take this and watch it on your own.', said Trish and gave the phone to Animesh.

'Whaaaaat?', said Animesh and his face turned all pale at that moment.

'What's happening guys?' I asked.

'Watch it on your own, I don't know how to break this up to you.', said Animesh and gave me the phone.

'What's there to be this dramatic about Ani?' I said and got up to snatch the phone from his hands out of annoyance. The very moment I looked at the screen, I freezed and lost all sense of how to react and respond. I was all numb. It was Sampat's picture there on the screen. He looked very different in that picture, completely different than how I saw him here today.. Today he looked all poised, a businessman with a particular rough behaviour, someone who is straight with his words and what he wants... There in that picture he looked just opposite.. chill sitting position wearing polaroid sunglasses with four to five unbuttoned shirt buttons having a huge smile over his face as if someone captured it when he was laughing. It was mentioned that he was suspected to be a mafia who was the sole mastermind of multiple murder, extortion, corruption, gambling, labor racketeering and stock manipulation schemes.

Notes

Where is the rest of the story?

Isn't this exactly what you are thinking right now?

Well!! The rest of the story is in "That Heart Still Behind A Beautiful Chaos"

Yes... It is the second part of "That Heart Behind A Beautiful Chaos"

So keep sipping on to your coffee and enjoy the journey cause we'll meet at our destination super soon.

-Dr. Sunaina Verma